THE COMPLETE TOVE JANSSON

MOOMIN

COMIC STRIP

Drawn & Quarterly

MONTRÉAL

Moomin Book One: The Complete Tove Jansson Comic Strip by Tove Jansson
ISBN 1-894937-80-5

Third Printing: June 2007
10 9 8 7 6 5 4 3

Printed in Singapore

Library and Archives Canada Cataloguing in Publication

Jansson, Tove
    Moomin : the complete Tove Jansson comic strip / Tove Jansson.

Originally published in the Evening News, London, 1953-1959.
ISBN 1-894937-80-5 (bk. 1)

    I. Title.

PN6738.M66J35 2006   741.5'94897   C2006-902218-6

Drawn & Quarterly
Post Office Box 48056
Montreal, Quebec
Canada H2V 4S8
www.drawnandquarterly.com

Distributed in the USA and abroad by:
Farrar, Straus and Giroux
19 Union Square West
New York, NY 10003
Orders: 888.330.8477

Distributed in Canada by:
Raincoast Books
9050 Shaughnessy Street
Vancouver, BC V6P 6E5
Orders: 800.663.5714

Distributed in the United Kingdom by:
Publishers Group U.K.
8 The Arena
Mollison Avenue
Enfield Middlesex EN3 7NL
Orders: 0208 804 0400

MOOMIN

VOLUME ONE

1. Moomin and the Brigands

23

2. Moomin and Family Life

41

3. Moomin on the Riviera

4. Moomin's Desert Island

Tove Jansson: To Live in Peace, Plant Potatoes, and Dream

Throughout her memoir *Sculptor's Daughter*, artist and author Tove Jansson describes a childhood environment much like that inhabited by the captivating characters in her Moomin comics—a magically ramshackle house filled with affectionate family, numerous friends, and a varied array of voracious guests—all set in the midst of a richly verdant seaside valley. After her birth in Helsinki in August of 1914, her family spent their summers along the shore, first at her grandparents' sprawling home on the archipelago of Stockholm, and later at her family's cottage near Porvoo on the Pellinge Islands of Finland. Her tender memories of these days are perhaps the most compelling motif within all of her works. Whether collecting pearly shells to line the flower beds, dragging errant treasures from the waves, or rubbing precious stream pebbles with margarine to make them glimmer, it was the ephemeral pleasures of nature and the company of loved ones that provided Jansson with her earliest inspiration.

Liberal and artistic parents also helped to kindle young Jansson's innate talents, and foster her often remarked upon tolerance for the idiosyncratic. As the eldest daughter of a sculptor, Viktor Jansson, and a graphic artist/illustrator, Signe Hammarsten-Jansson, Tove was immersed in a creative and often raucously eccentric household. A pet monkey named Poppolino, who was reputedly fond of wearing argyle sweaters, and a nanny who read Plato were only two of the less than conventional members of this extended Jansson "family," and it was most likely these peculiar but beloved figures who became the models for the dreamers, philosophers, and dilettantes who populate her fictional world. In the Valley of the Moomins, whether it be Moominmamma's soothing, homespun wisdom or Sniff's egocentric desire for wealth and fame, everyone's unique perspective is accorded equal consideration. These whimsically drawn creatures are comically human, and Jansson's emotionally rich but often fiscally impoverished bohemianism is probably reflected in the Moomin's sensual frivolity. Tiny bikinis, shimmery chandeliers, whiskey, jewels, and roses are evidence of the importance of relishing the moment, a maxim Jansson was said to have followed most of her life.

The smell of wet plaster and sight of a father sculpting away at his modeling clay, as well as the diligence of a mother who read every book she illustrated so that she would have the proper feel, and thus look, of a character, were Jansson's formative images of her parents' devotion to their art, and it was only natural that she followed their lead. At the age of fifteen, she published her first drawings in the politically progressive *Garm* magazine, and soon after left for the Konstfack art academy in Stockholm. At nineteen, she continued her studies at the Helsinki Art Society's drawing school at the Finnish National Gallery, while concurrently traveling around the continent and exhibiting both abroad and in Finland. In 1938 Jansson took yet further lessons in Paris at both the Ecole d'Adrien Holy and Ecole des Beaux Arts, and by the end of the decade, she was recognized as one of Finland's most gifted young artists. The vanity and vacuity of the modern art world are certainly mirrored in the first volume of *Moomin*, and Jansson lampoons her own romantic nature. When Sniff instructs poor Moomintroll to create art that is "baffling" and "bewildering," as surely that will earn them riches, his happy go lucky, tubby-tummied friend answers that he wants only to "live in peace, plant potatoes and dream!" Tove Jansson knew all too well that a velvet beret doesn't make one an artist, and soon returned home to Finland for good.

It was in the pages of *Garm* in 1940 that Jansson first introduced Moomintroll as a sort of signature figure within her illustrations. In 1945, his charming family was introduced in her first children's book, *Småtrollen och den Stora Översvämningen* (*The Little Trolls and the Great Flood*), although it was the third in the series, *Trollkarlens Hatt* (*The Magician's Hat*, or as titled in English, *Finn Family Moomintroll*) that captured the widest readership and affirmed her lifelong reputation as an adored children's author. In the early 1950s, the Associated Press in England contacted Jansson about turning her beloved trolls' escapades into a comic strip for adults. Having already drawn a successful comic exploit titled *Mumintrollet och jordens undergång* (*Moomintrolls and the End of the World*) for *Ny Tid*, a Finland-Swedish newspaper, Jansson took them up on their proposal. In 1953 the *London Evening News* began running *Moomin* on a daily basis, and it was soon published in over 40 papers around the world. Jansson drew the strip for five years, until she realized that the grueling schedule of a daily and being creative on demand did not suit her meandering attitude towards life. As one of her fictional alter-egos, Mymble, instructs those who worry and fret: "Lie on the bridge and watch the water flowing past. Or run, or wade through the swamp in your red boots. Or roll yourself up and listen to the rain falling on the roof. It's very easy to enjoy yourself."

In addition to the ten children's novels, which have been translated into 34 languages, three whimsical picture books, and the comics collected in these volumes, Jansson was passionately prolific in her other artistic pursuits, writing a number of poetic, often bittersweet, novels for adults, as well as painting vividly engaging murals for such public institutions as the Aurora Children's Hospital in Helsinki. Her devotion to a life of creativity and imagination did not go unrewarded, and she received a number of significant prizes for her work: among these are the Nils Holgersson plaquette in 1953, the esteemed Hans Christian Andersen medal in 1966, the Swedish Academy prize in 1972, the Pro Finlandia medal in 1976, and on multiple occasions, the Finnish State prize for literature. Six years before her death in 2001, the eighty year old Jansson was awarded the honorary title of professor at the Åbo Akademi University in 1995, a fitting tribute for a vital woman who taught the world some of life's most fundamental lessons: float on clouds, wear red boots, and always, always, live in peace.

—Alisia Grace Chase, PhD